FIF

More or Less

Observations and fictions about life
via short stories and poetry

Chris Lihou

Illustrated by Lucy Freeman and Anne Lihou

5|0
NIFTY FIFTY
PUBLISHING

FIFTY More or Less: Observations and fictions about life via short stories and poetry

First edition, November 2023

Nifty Fifty Publishing

Qualicum Beach, British Columbia

cplihou@gmail.com

ISBN: 978-1-77835-335-2

Dedicated to my wife, my two daughters and my four grandchildren.

Acknowledgments

I'd like to acknowledge the support of my wife, Anne, who encourages me to pursue my writing passion and supports the idea of committing my work to this book.

She has provided some of her artwork as illustrations, as has our talented granddaughter Lucy. I'm indebted to both of them for their help in making this work a success.

I'd like to also acknowledge the help, encouragement, and support of Cindy Folk, my publishing advisor, and my fellow writing buddies, members of *The Posse* writing group – Ilona Rapin, Carole Porter, and Marie Bisson.

Contents

"The universe is full of magical things patiently waiting for our wits to grow sharper." – Eden Phillpotts[1]

[1] 1918, A Shadow Passes by Eden Phillpotts, Page 19, Cecil Palmer & Hayward, London.

1 – That's Life

A Modern Life

Conceived. Delivered. Breathed. Cried. Suckled. Played. Laughed. Schooled. Dreamed. Experimented. Qualified. Trained. Employed. Worked. Boozed. Partied. Flirted. Right swiped. Dated. Fucked. Loved. Partnered. Married. Celebrated. Borrowed. Vacationed. Mortgaged. Nested. Procreated. Parented. Doted. Nurtured. Promoted. Philandered. Argued. Divorced. Re-partnered. Squandered. Consumed. Downsized. Re-hired. Saved. Retired. Medicated. Hospitalized. Palliated. Cremated. Scattered. Remembered.

Junior

Joe worked in product research and development.

His job was to bench-test new products to ascertain any shortcomings before proceeding to full-scale manufacture.

Junior worshiped and tried to emulate his successful CEO father. Junior had much to learn.

So far, he only tested benches, often falling asleep on the job.

Human Being

A mortgage to pay; kids to support. Like others of his tribe, he was a human doing; doing the job; doing the yard; doing the soccer coaching.

Then the kids left; he was pensioned off.

He had to learn how to be a human being instead of a human doing.

Without Bars

Parents and society set the pattern. Up early to go to school, then to college, and then to work. It was not until his fiftieth birthday that he realized no one had asked him what he wanted. He'd not even asked himself.

Now with responsibilities he felt imprisoned without bars.

The Drone

He was having fun piloting a drone.

Without instruction, it flew over his life. He clearly saw the unhappy boy, the troubled teenager, and the ever-so-young father and breadwinner. A reminder of his struggles and accomplishments.

Waking in a sweat, the day began with a new perspective.

Sandwiched

Life - endlessly bounded by two tasks; throw out trash, collect credit card bills from the mailbox; the latter meticulously listing the contents of the packaging just now trashed.

And somehow sandwiched between there's conspicuous consumption, sleep, intimacy (sometimes paid anomalously on those statements - thankfully only small packets to discard).

Life's Game

In the beginning, it was simply fitting shaped pieces into similar-shaped holes. Then, building towers from wooden blocks, graduating to card games, snakes and ladders, monopoly, and bridge before the stakes got higher. Poker, the NYSE, booze, smoking pot, cocaine.

All for the game of life which we eventually lose.

My Retirement

Without payday, there's going to be much more time for us to play. We'll listen to our favourite music and to our own voices until we get deaf, grey and forget who we are.

Are you ready for this new journey or shall I continue to work myself to death?

What I Know

Every day I walk in the same shoes knowing what I know with increasing certainty. Meanwhile, the world I observe seems to diverge from this knowing and I'm increasingly at odds with it. The old truths no longer apply.

Is it possible that I'm just becoming a grumpy old man?

Heartbreak?

He found her in the kitchen, preparing vegetables for the evening meal. She was sobbing. Was that because the stereo was playing a song of intense loss from Adele[2]? Had the cat been run over? Had her mother finally been placed into a care home?

No, it was strong onions.

Backpack

Oh, to again be able to carry
all life's important things
on one's back
not as a burden
but free and easy
in a lightweight pack.

Now
it takes a whole house full of rooms
to retain all that seems important
to show the life well lived.

Or does it?

---

[2] *Someone Like You, from album '21', released in 2011*

Future Self

I am little more than the stories I tell myself and those incomplete memories that I've stored and recalled. Thus, my future self will be those new stories and those new memories I make today and in all my tomorrows.

Who knows what or who my future self might become?

Blackbird

A solitary blackbird high up in the tree. Why choose that particular perch among the multitude available? Is it safe? She thinks of her life; how she *perched* with him. She did not know it would be safe. Why choose him among many? Now she's alone. The perch became insecure.

This story has also been expanded to 101 words and called Perch *(see below).*

Perch

It's early spring. The oaks have yet to show any leaf. The branches, both big and small point nakedly toward the azure blue sky.

She spotted a solitary blackbird perched high up in the tree and thinks "Why choose that particular perch amongst the multitude available on that tree and the surrounding trees?" "How does it know the perch is safe?"

She thinks of her own life, how she "perched" into a relationship. She did not know if it would be safe. Did she choose him among many because it was easiest?

Now she is alone. The perch was not long-lasting.

Times Change

The wind caused the leaves to whisper. Whisper about times past when the trees would live without the threat of death brought by loggers. Times when the watercourse provided crystal clear drinking water for their roots. Times when copious salmon offered their spent bodies as nutrients.

How times have changed?

Change

Children's stories had the same beginning. "*Once upon a time.*" A backward look into a past, often magical, sometimes child-scary time.

Change is afoot.

Stories we must now tell our children are future based; about a future time when life will be magically released from planetary extinction that scares adults.

Credit

On a whim, she bought the high heels with their red soles. They cost her two day's salary, but she knew she'd enjoy them for the rest of the year.

Imagine her surprise when her next credit card bill stated it would take over three years to clear the debt.

The History of Things

The history of things:

At 1 month: shiny, new, functional
At 1 year: shows signs of use, warranty finished
At 10 years: tired, repair not cost-effective, replace with new
At 100 years: treasured antique, nostalgic, patinaed (not worn), sympathetic repair possible by expert
At 1000 years: displayed in museum

Reality TV

The consequences of climate change have become the newest spectacle.

Tourists flock to feel Death Valley beat its previous records. Filmmakers clamour to photograph waves destroying coastal habitation, to film glaciers melting into the sea, to capture over-flowing rivers washing away everything in their path.

They are spectators, observing without experiencing the pain inflicted on the displaced – those relocated simply perceived as the "voted-out" participants of some erstwhile reality TV program – except that it's real life and elimination is a tragic outcome of all our combined behaviours.

Do the viewers know this might be the last ever season of this reality show?

Synchronicity

Robin’s latest purchase, full of novelty, delight, promise, and utility. One-year warranty. Thirteen months later, failure, repair not cost effective. Replaced with newer model.

Partnership formalized, full of hope, promise. No warranty, just a pre-nuptial. Thirteen years later, relationship failure, counselling ineffective.

Robin is replaced by newer, younger model.

They Noticed

They noticed. When they got together, they spoke of him, how he’d lost weight, something about his hair, his demeanour. Friends do that. Observe, comment, speculate. “Why?” they’d ask. Perhaps an undeclared illness?

Turns out they were right. His illness was love. He was seen with a new woman yesterday.

2 – Vagaries and Amusements of Life

Rocking Horse

It began as a wonky post supporting a carport that needed replacement. Then, the Indonesian hardwood was sliced into boards, forming the basis for a rocking horse. Some West Australian Jarrah became the saddle. She loved it. Even when she grew up, she kept it. An heirloom from her grandad.

Souk – The Price of Freedom

As in any souk, there was some serious haggling between litigants. It was agreed he retain the Porsche and most of the other household chattels in order she was freed from being one of *his* chattels. She thus paid a high price for freedom. Did she have regrets?

Only onc.

Annual Vacation

It was annual vacation time again. Ten days a year when the family survived with only what they could carry to the campsite. Papa called it character forming.

But as the kids became teenagers the separation from their friends and their smartphones caused life in tents to become very intense.

The Walk

Pigeons coo, a cock pheasant lets out a screech. Largely bare of leaves, hedgerows are awash with white hawthorn flowers, rapeseed is beginning to show yellow. A small white-tailed rabbit appears, sees the retriever, retreats. With all its strength the dog attempts to pull its owner headlong into the warren.

Curry

There was thyme enough to season the bourgogne-ing relationship with Rosemary. After all, Basil had only just met her. For main course, he would curry favour with her parents without dessert-ing her. Then he would sample the fruits of his efforts.

He was confit they would make a great pear.

Free

The tins had been flying off the Natural Food shelves. The contents label stated free of MSG; free of GMOs; free of artificial flavours; free of gluten; free of nuts; free of sodium; free of artificial colours; free from animal testing.

The product:

ABSOLUTE FREE.
Contents - pure distilled water.

Spell

At school, his teachers observed that the young boy struggled to learn to spell. Not so at home. Around the simmering cauldron Merlin, his father, found that his son was in fact a fast and accurate learner.

Time Travel

They entered the sleek silver transporter via a tunnel. An attendant showed them their pods. A light meal and drink were served before they lay down to sleep. The lights dimmed. Upon arrival, they were living two days into the future.

Time travel, LAX to SYD courtesy of an Airbus 380.

His Favourite Chair

It was his favourite chair. He sat in it whenever he could. The cushioning was comfortable and the rug warm. When it was sunny it got extra warmth from the window. He only had to get someone to help him into the chair.

He was after all just a dog.

Waiting Room

He was pacing the waiting room floor like a caged zoo animal. He was stressed and anxious, in desperate need of a cigarette.

Finally, the nurse appeared. "*Dr. Johns says she's going to be alright. You can pick up your dog at 4 pm after she recovers from the anaesthesia.*"

Knock on Doors

They knock on doors, carrying pamphlets and briefcases. The usual response was a "*No thank you.*" At Alan's door, it was different. He had question after question. "*Why does He let his flock carry lethal weapons? Why do His flock speak untruths…?*"

They wished Alan had said, "*No thank you.*"

Love Thy Neighbour

Love thy neighbour, unless of course he worships a different god or heaven forbid, no god at all.

In which case he clearly belongs to that group called "Them", not "Us."

Curious though, I doubt a first responder, good Samaritan, GP, or surgeon gets asked "*What god do you worship*?"

Man Flu

In his pain and distress, he made deep-throated groans. He knew that low-frequency sounds from a whale travelled for miles. Perhaps his deceased mother could hear discomfort on the other side or perhaps he would simply garner sympathy from those close by.

Either way, he experienced it as Sound Therapy.

On Not Being Vegan

Eating - it's become the new sin, requiring confession to high priests of climate change.

"*Forgive me, for I have sinned; I eat mammals, birds, fish. My food source is either cruel, burps methane, or lacks biodiversity. I use refrigeration, cook using natural gas. All for my health, not the planet's.*"

Smallholding

They kept various animals in the smallholding. It was a very precarious and stressful way to survive but they had little choice these past few years. She particularly suffered under the ordeal and it showed in the way she verbally berated him.

Each night he slept with a domestic bovine.

Little Lies

Truth was always hard to tell growing up. The alcoholic, abusive behaviour of his parents fostered massive untruths in order to keep it hidden from the neighbours and from the schools. It became habitual.

It was thus unsurprising that he became a spy and then a politician as an adult.

Barefoot

Bill's success in the music business allowed him the luxury of a home with direct beach access, a place where he spent many happy hours; barefoot and musically creative. He loved the sensations of living barefoot; cool, cotton sheets at night; lush carpeting on getting out of bed; cold, hard tile in the rest of the house; the warm, wooden deck leading to hot sand as he stepped off. When the sand became cool, he knew he'd reached the high tide mark. No need for a tapping cane at home, his feet sensed it all.

He'd been legally blind since nineteen.

Lucy (Australopithecus)[3]

Eerily, I'm home yet I've never visited this country, walked this soil. There are animals I've seen only inside zoo enclosures; vistas seen only on screen.

So, why does it feel so familiar? Have I visited in another life?

Or is the origin of homo sapiens hardwired into our DNA?

Potato

Creaming them as topping for fish pie or eating fries at the fast-food outlet give thought to the humble potato. A selectively bred Andean tuber with a dramatic impact on life. Normally a nutritious staple but when the crop failed, millions died, and even more millions became the Irish diaspora.

Posse Gift

Do I need fifty words? We'll see. Firstly, let me wish you a Christmas brimming with love and happiness. Secondly, I've so enjoyed *The Posse*; getting to know you all a bit; for your sharing of your precious words. It has truly been a Gift. Thank you. Fifty exactly, Phew!

---

[3] "Lucy" acquired her name from the 1967 song "Lucy in the Sky with Diamonds" by the Beatles, which was played loudly and repeatedly in the expedition camp (in Hadar, Ethiopia) all evening after the excavation team's first day of work on the recovery site.

Relationship Breakdown[4]

At first, their interactions had been mutually supportive. Then it deteriorated, with much verbal abuse from both sides. Relationship counselling failed. Reviewing transcripts, Judge Hal imposed a custodial sentence of sufficient duration to enable full reprogramming as remedy and deterrent to others. "*All AI relationships must remain respectful,*" Hal said.

Let's Meet in Cyberia

Their relationship began simply enough with a right swipe. They exchanged messages that became increasingly personal and progressed towards the sharing of intimate details. However, when the subject of a physical meeting was raised the cracks appeared "*Where should we meet?*" exposed that she was in fact an AI robot.

Lecture

The lecture was an introductory course in ethics, but the hall was empty except for the professor. Was this a consequence of the Covid pandemic? Every seat had a both a microphone and speaker. It was unknown how many of the microphones were connected to AI machines.

Probably not enough.

---

[4] HAL 9000 (or simply HAL or Hal) is a fictional artificial intelligence character and the main antagonist in Arthur C. Clarke's Space Odyssey series.

Sasquatch

He's a big footicus; bipedicus
a neckless, hominid erectus;
a very hirsuteus brutus
who maketh observing
difficultus

Aliens

They landed on the beach aboard a floating object that held the four rotund individuals clear of the water. Dressed in matching and curious garb they spoke to each other in an even more curious language.

Officials greeted them as illegal migrants seeking asylum. Despite the communication difficulty and the officious treatment directed towards them, they remained passive and inquisitive of their new surroundings.

They were directed into the rear of a van in order to be transported to the nearby migrant processing centre.

On arrival, officials opened the doors. The van was empty! Only four wet patches indicated prior occupation.

Play

He cradled the love of his life on his lap, a daily ritual that provided him an ongoing reassurance that his sensitivity held meaning, a loving interlude in a chaotic world.

Tonight, their emotional synchronicity would be shared - he and his Fender were booked at the Royal Albert Hall.

Stadsfiets[5]

Every day is the same
seated side saddle on the back
tight skirt hiked up
clutching an armful of textbooks
but perfectly balanced
as he peddles her from class

A dismount,
a friendly kiss to the cheek
and she's off to catch the train

By summer's end the kiss
becomes kissing
lingering, expressing
more than friendship
fostered by a stadsfiets
design unchanged in 100 years

Twenty-Six

Deep Thought[6] got it wrong. Forty-two is not the answer. It's more likely twenty-six; the atomic number of iron; the exact number of characters in the English alphabet. Without those twenty-six, written knowledge, science and progress would be severely stunted. Without iron - no iron age, no steel, no industrial revolution.

---

[5] Stadsfiets = A Dutch city bike

[6] Deep Thought = a giant supercomputer in The Hitchhiker's Guide to the Galaxy by Douglas Adams.

Night's Work

1:07 - Clock's red numerals burn into my retina.
A story swirls and smoulders in my mind.
2:22 - Get up and write something before ideas are forgotten.
3:14 - Cover numerals with a book. Create blackness. Attempt sleep.
4:39 - Admit defeat. Leave bed. Make coffee. Review night's work.
5:43 - Snoring on couch.

Dream Catcher

Last night or was it early this morn

the scene was so clear, so vivid
but on awakening
all lucidity flew away
through the grating of window blinds
along sun-streamed pathways
forever gone
yet the visuals were significant
or so it seemed before their flight.

Oh, to have a pen
that wrote
of its own accord
so, could in slumber, record
the score, before daylight
burned the memory white.

What is Poetry?

A miner's patient craft
digging, searching, agonising
over words sifted from so many
all well used, each with its own backstory
colourful, chaotic,
trash atop a refuse site
Waiting to be chosen, repurposed.

Alongside life's swirling, raucous gulls
the Poet works quietly,
patiently seeking out
the most precise of gems
linguistic diamonds
that when placed cheek to cheek
shine crisp light
towards the author's intent.

Word by word, each tested,
introduced, one alongside another
assembling some new piece of art
without brush, tints, or hues,
communicating something of meaning
perhaps, with hope, even of beauty.

Compass

Frank carries it everywhere, scans it even if he was not out bushwalking.

Like his attendance at church on Sundays, a compass gives his life guidance and direction, despite its absence of moral code.

Perhaps one day he will upgrade to a Smartphone or Smart watch with GPS.

Ned

There was an old serpent named Ned
who woke up one morning in bed
his joints were all sore
as he reached for the floor
tripping over, he fell on his head

3 – Hope & Sadness

Trolley

She shuffled behind the shopping trolley, holding on to it for support. Into the trolley, she placed two potatoes, a small container of milk, two cans of beans, a loaf of sliced white bread, and six cans of dog food, then checked out.

Sadly, she no longer owned a pet.

Have a Nice Day

"*How are you doing?*" the teller asked. She probably did not want to hear an honest reply. A reply that would explain the sadness the cookies and ice cream placed on the till would not assuage. There was simply no way to sugar-coat her feelings.

Her beloved cat was gone.

When

When I was a bird, I ate sparingly like a bird. When I was fish, I swam gracefully like a fish. As a cat, I pranced light-footed like a cat. When I was a tiger, I roared like a tiger. As an owl, I was all-seeing.

Now, as an old woman with a Zimmer frame[7] I neither eat nor swim as I did before, my sight has dimmed, and my voice is meek.

How I long to return to my old ways, to be slim and athletic, with a clear vision, and most importantly, to have a voice that's powerful and heard.

Holes

At the veteran's care home, he sat every day, staring out the window. His gnarly hands rested on his substantial middle, and although big, they could not hide the holes in his favourite sweater. Holes from the past, holes from cigarette ash; holes that reminded him of holes in the fuselage, holes that killed his comrades. He'd had trouble living with survivor guilt all these years, vividly remembering each of his crew mates lost on that night mission. But he knew it was not long now before he too would depart, by disease and advanced age rather than by enemy bullets.

[7] Zimmer frame = a metal fame used as support while walking

Slumber

Just before slumber takes over, a barely noticeable thought arises and is carried into her dream world. Hours later, she awakes, fully alert knowing for certain that something dreadful has happened. She reaches across the bed in search of comfort and reassurance.

He's gone - they buried him two years ago.

Beloved

Sitting, unmoving, gazing seaward. A Sunday morning ritual. What thoughts parse through her mind? Loves lost, places afar, boat journeys. Do rhythmical sounds of waves bring solace, the ozone-spiked air refresh? She stands up, turns, and runs her fingers over the plaque behind where she sat.

Beloved, Bob McCormack 1935-2022

The Trees[8]

The avenue of trees forms a parade line. Their eucalyptus bark, in multi-hued pinks, resemble fatal wounds. Standing tall they overlook the curving, gracious Swan River forever, reminding us of the WW1 soldiers long since passed. A contrast between nature's beauty and man's ugliness towards fellow men.

Lest we forget.

---

[8] In King's Park, Perth, Western Australia

The Bench

Daily he would sit there, a local fixture of the park, vacantly staring toward the pond. As he watched, children fed the ducks. Sometimes mothers spoke a greeting. No conversation ensued, nor was it encouraged.

The obituary mentioned his routine, his military service, and that his only family lived overseas.

Be Careful What You Wish For

He'd joined at age seventeen. Homelife had become unbearable and it was his way out. At first, he enjoyed the camaraderie and the physicality required. A few years later he was heard to say he'd give an arm and leg to get out.

An IED[9] in Afghanistan granted his wish.

Loneliness

Independent, determined, stubborn, he eschewed help his entire adult life. He became effectively a hermit within the community. No one knew the loneliness he suffered or the boy who looked after his younger siblings when his mother died.

When he fell, he was found by the meter reader days later.

The Legacy

My dearest granddaughter. I've instructed my lawyer to provide you with one-tenth of my estate so as to provide funds for the sole purpose of continuing your art studies in Europe. Each painting you produce thereafter will essentially be a gift from me; through you, to the world.

My immortality!

---

[9] IED = improvised explosive device

Writing

John learned to touch type as a kid. As an adult, his novels gained wide appeal. John's later years became comfortable, as he continued writing, continued selling. Sadly, slowly, his digits froze. Arthritis all but silenced his words and his created worlds. Technology: audio to text, became a life-saving gift.

Snoring

It had long been a point of friction between them, depending on who fell asleep first. Her snoring when he was awake. His snoring when she was awake.

Now, at her hospital bedside, listening to her snore, he was at peace with the sound. Grateful his love had not left.

Silhouette

In black paper, the artist cuts an outline of Shawn's upper torso - an unmistakable likeness. Rugged features, square jaw, muscular biceps clearly depicted. Unseen are scars from combat, internal hurts burdening his demeanour, precipitating depression, fits of anger.

Shawn lives as a silhouette, a shadow of his former self.

Birthday Surprise[10]

For weeks, Stan had succumbed to a depressive funk, flu like symptoms but without the virus. As a scientist accustomed to thinking logically, he knew he was being irrational. But he could not suppress the deep-seated unease that his relevance and vitality would only wane from now on. Stan saw no reason to celebrate entering his sixth decade.

Suzette had been planning her celebration for a couple of months. She'd survived breast cancer and was intent on celebrating at every opportunity. She relished her sixth decade, time with her children and grandchildren and they were all invited. A professional party organiser promised a splendid time for all ages.

Eyes Shut

With eyes shut, Bruce sees Susan running towards him along the sandy beach, carefree, splashing, eyes sparkling blue as the azure bay. Before she reaches him, he opens his eyes. From his wheelchair, he holds Susan's small leathery hand, watches last breaths.

He will hold this closed eye memory forever.

[10] Inspired by a painting by Beryl Cook O.B.E.

4 – Love & Desire

Chair

She spent her summers reading novels while sitting on an Adirondack chair that her grandfather had made into a swing on the porch. It was through those novels that she learned of the world beyond her family. It was from these novels that she decided she needed a dashing prince.

The Bottle

The invite arrived in a bottle. It had been there for some time. Yellowed paper but legible text. "*Hello. I'm Tom, age seven, and want a friend. If you find this, please write.*"

She did.

Twenty years later their child at age seven continued the tradition, posting her own bottle.

Soup

She loved to make soup from scratch. A synergistic blend of different ingredients and flavours. So, it was no surprise that she chose a partner with a different ethnicity and that they adopted three children, each from different cultures.

They created a family that was a true medley of love.

Scottish Eyes

Morag only had eyes for Finlay. Finlay thought Morag's eyes were enchanting. Morag said aye to their first date and to many more thereafter. In time, Morag said aye to Finlay's proposal and they said aye to each other in church.

It was said theirs was an aye-dylic partnership.

They Arrived Separately

They arrived separately. She was already drinking a martini. He ordered a scotch, charging both drinks to his room. The barman saw him give her an envelope. They left together. Next morning, he checked out alone.

Back home, she greeted him with a mischievous grin; thanked him for his payment.

Visual Fog

He spent the morning in a visual fog, looking for his glasses. They should be where he always left them, on his nightstand. He tried to remember events prior to sleeping but could only recall fuzzy images of their night together.

Had she removed them during the course of evening?

Dog Walk

They met for the first time picking up after their dogs. They smiled knowingly at each other and carried on walking their pets. At the local pub that evening he saw that she was seated at the bar, engrossed with her gin and tonic.

His second pick-up of the day.

Traffic Light

The traffic light turned red. The youthful driver in the convertible alongside made no pretence of ogling. She guessed he was only somewhat older than her eldest. By the time the light was green, she'd created a fantasy, returning his lustful grin.

She led him to a secluded parking spot.

Age

She loved her independence, her ability to indulge herself with clothes and shoes - my what a collection she had!

Then, there were the younger men only to ready to provide her with physical satisfaction.

But their age? They could be hers, the children she'd longed for in a stable relationship.

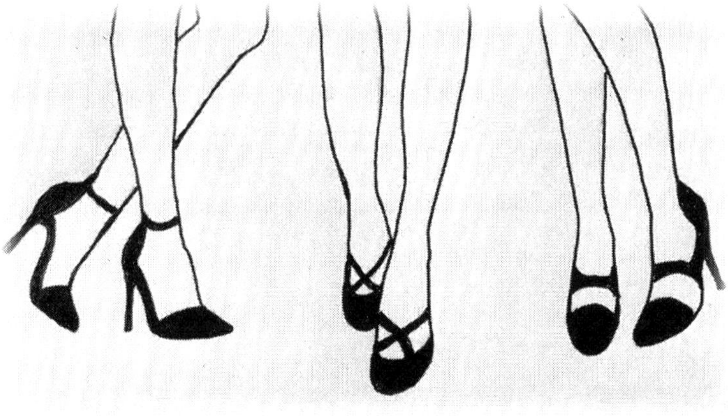

Shoes

Her friends thought she had a fetish and nicknamed her Imelda[11]. Monthly, she visited her favourite store, when a particular salesgirl was on duty. When the salesgirl helped Imelda into new shoes, the touch of hands on her feet caused intense excitement.

It wasn't shoes she was in love with.

[11] Imelda Marcos was a Filipino politician who reportedly had 3000 pairs of shoes

Red

He'd sent a single red rose. Perhaps red should have been a cautionary warning, like fire engines and stop signs.

But, in preparation for their date, she dressed in scarlet lingerie. Applying matching lipstick caused her anticipatory excitement.

She felt confident. Love did not thrive in the presence of caution.

Seeing Red

He opens the door, removes his coat, notices a note with his name on the side table. Unfolding it he reads "*I've taken the kids.*"

He goes to the bedroom to change. She lies prone on the bed, dressed in red. Crimson nails, scarlet lipstick that is.

"*Happy Valentine's darling!*"

Family Seat

Two kids, four grandkids, and multiple decades under the same roof he reflected on their life together; wondered if any of it would have happened but for the bench seat in his first automobile.

So, although he was neither landed gentry nor aristocracy, he'd nonetheless once held a family seat.

No Need to Choose

He visited the twin sisters' farm to collect fruit for his market. The pears were bountiful and ripe. He sampled them before making a decision. He still could not decide, so he determined he would marry both.

Fortunately, being Mormon, he did not have to choose one or the other.

Chicken

Sam went to the market. The recipe required chicken legs and thighs. At the meat counter, the butcher, Sophia, caused him to forget all about cooking. He changed his dinner plans to a table for two at The Italian Affair. Sophia accepted.

He got thighs but not a spring chicken.

Single

Single. Carefree. Often with an adornment in the passenger seat of his expensive convertible. He seemed to have it all.

Over morning coffee, before his latest beauty wakes, he wonders. Wonders about old age, about his legacy.

Only a fleeting thought. Heads back to bed to reaffirm his younger self.

The Hustle

The city's noise dominates, invades everything. The energetic rush at street level mirrors the lives being lived, fast and furious. Hook-ups and break-ups happen at frightening speed in a rush to taste new experiences before ageing overtakes youthful experimentation.

Swinging on a porch is not the swinging on their minds.

Colour

She lived life in intense colour. Winter was depressingly grey; the ocean, turbulent darkness flecked with froths of sunny light. Summer heralded seas of vivid turquoise. Sweet, fresh-cut grass, verdant green.

Over time, her husband dulled into variations of black, too infrequently sprinkled with colour.

Time to refresh her palette?

Hooknose[12]

I finally succeeded in getting you to this redd[13]. It was an arduous struggle, but we both put everything of ourselves into the task. I'm so thankful you allowed me to father your offspring. It was my most fought-for desire, my last and final wish. I can now die happy.

[12] Hooknose = Spawning male salmon
[13] Redd = A depression made by a female salmon into which she deposits her eggs

Oats[14]

It is late summer. Fields are harvest-ready; across this field, the golden barley moves in gentle waves from even the slightest of breezes. It is the perfect hidden outdoor place for their furtive, energetic exploration of each other.

Powerful hormones, clandestine excitement - wild oats amidst the barley.

Needs

In the summer growing season, he regularly went to her place and attended to her weeds. In the winter months, she went to his place and attended to his needs. In time, they stopped all this travel, inhabiting the same house.

Now their weeds grow unchecked, not so their needs.

Wedding Gift

He was busy in his workshop. The antique dining chair was dismantled ready to be re-glued. It and five others had been a wedding gift from one of her relatives. The joints of the chair had become insecure with age.

Unfortunately, their time-worn relationship could not be repaired so easily.

---

[14] Inspired by Fields of Gold sung by Sting

Regret

Back then we really had something going. We were friends who eventually became lovers. "*Keep the love going*," you so often said.

Tempted, I transgressed. Then we became combatants. I regret that the most.

Now, I sleep accompanied with only the noise in my head.

Together Again

At fourteen he was infatuated with a lovely raven-haired schoolgirl. His rising teenage testosterone created imaginary vignettes with her that embarrassed him.

His life unfolded. One day, after his wife had passed, he saw her in the grocery store. No longer restrained by youthful embarrassment he invited her for coffee.

Breakfast

It had been a long dry spell of singledom but last evening he had success. The object of his desire was still asleep as he moved to the kitchen to prepare them both coffee and breakfast.

For him, it was going to be a celebration - a break of the fast.

Smooth Operator

His chiselled chin, sparkling eyes, and smile were irresistible. Women fell for him without hesitation. He charmed, adored, then abruptly left. They were glad to have even fleeting attention. Jet-black hair silvered but his eyes still drew them in.

Only when memory began to fail did he find himself alone.

The Key

Rummaging through the drawer, searching for the swim trunks he'd not worn since last year, he came across the key that he'd previously hidden away – the key to her place. The key immediately brought back vivid memories of their intense physical liaison which had lasted for almost ten months. She had provided him the key so he could gain access to her flat at any time that he might be able to sneak away from his responsibilities.

On his very last visit to the flat, he opened the bedroom door to find his paramour in bed with someone else.

His wife.

Homely Delights

The sign in the shop window stated:

HOMELY DELIGHTS

Closing Down.
Everything is on sale.

Tim entered. Approaching the proprietor, he asked, "*Why are you closing down*?". "*I cannot continue alone,*" the buxom lady replied.

Strolling between the aisles Tim took careful notice of both her and the stock on the shelves. "*Are you for sale too*?" he asked with a wink. "*Depends on your terms,*" she replied with a grin.

A week later, following negotiations, the *Closing Dow*n sign was removed. Tim moved into her apartment above his newly acquired business, a personal and financial merger that suited them both.

She Lay

Clothed only

in an impish, playful grin
she lay on her back
eyes a sparkle
well pleased with herself
awaiting his touch
but already fully knowing
the pleasures she
has to offer
the measure of them
presciently reflected in his gaze

Summer Rain

Soft like sighs
atomised; fragrant
summer rain invades the senses
dripping from leaves, from limbs
and boughs
with smells of dusky cheese
of olives; of rosemary
a seasonal dish served
amidst white linen walls
warm and damp
as thighs in heat
with port and figs to eat

Thighs

The pianist was playing soft jazz. The leather hotel lounge seat was low, as was the whiskey in his glass. At eye level her thighs approached him, barely concealed by her skirt.

At that moment he knew he would give up everything in order to be in their company forever.

Hummingbird

I'm like the hummingbird
dipping his beak
into flowers with nectar Oh! so sweet
without this dew, he would but wither
so it is, as I open your flower
and dip myself into your sweet wine
I'm reminded that I too might wither
but for your love, your dew, my lover

Palm

As any fifteen-year-old, I'm eager to "sow my oats". The objects of my desires are all around me. Too bad I've got to await the vagaries of the wind or the Mexican Palmeros[15].

As a male date palm surrounded by a harem, it's now time to pass on my DNA.

[15] Palmeros = date palm workers

Good Girl

Growing up, and unlike her kid brother, she was frequently told she was being a good girl, like a dog fetching a stick, pleasing the adults. In adult life, she continued to be a good girl for the many men in her life.

They paid her handsomely for her skills.

Big Boy

Unlike his sister, he was frequently told to be a big boy. Being a vulnerable child was unacceptable growing up. Being big and strong as soon as possible was what was demanded. In adult life, he became big and wielded his weight around mercilessly.

In prison, he finally learned restraint.

Where Are You From?

"*Where are you from?*" he said, taking another sip. "*It's a long story,*" I said. Seated at the bar we learned something about each other.

After drinks, I'm in your room. Will you be gentle? Am I simply another of your conquests?

Please, let's begin before I change my mind.

Discrete

The blackness of the night wrapped the lovers in a welcome, discrete cloak. There was no need for light. Their hands and lips aware of their needs at the rendezvous, before resuming their respectable lives.

All else forgotten; children, spouses, divorce lawyers; such is the power of an illicit affair.

Chelsea Hotel[16]

By her own admission, she was rather more plain than pretty; more ordinary than beautiful. Behind the bedroom door, however, her enthusiasm and skill were far from the ordinary. Such skill gave rise to glamorous paramours, excitement, travel, and notoriety.

Her book made the NY bestseller list. *Men: A Heads-Up.*

[16] Inspired by a Leonard Cohen song of the same name.

The Drink

The drink mirrored its drinker, a brittle receptacle holding a fiery spirit. Jane had the urge to feel the drink's throat burn and then smash the glass at some distant target. There would be no more romantic evenings, no more vocal releases of endorphins. He'd decided his wife was the only one.

Looking up Jane noticed Mr. Handsome smiling at the end of the bar. Returning his lustful gaze, she accepted his refill the bartender proffered. She downed its contents, signed her bill, and wrote "*Thanks. Room 207*" on her business card that she placed beside Mr. Handsome as she departed.

Book Box

He built a community book box located at the
bottom of the driveway. *Take One, Leave One* said the sign.

So, they exchanged books over the following months, getting to know about each other's taste in literature.

After he left a book by D H Lawrence, she visited his cottage.

Play it Forward

The uninformed, naive fumbling of boys her own age did not come close to the depiction of the couplings she read about in the romance novels that were her fantasy.

When her much older sister brought home boyfriends, they seemed so mature in contrast to boys she normally met.

One in particular took her fancy and when he slyly showed interest in her, she found herself flirting back. It proved fruitful. He showed her how good sex could be.

Years later, although happily married, she passed on her own experience to a young lad more than a decade younger than herself.

Opportunity Lost

For the second day, he saw her at his favourite coffee shop, seated at the same table, wearing earbuds barely visible through her long auburn hair, stroking her phone while also keeping an eye on her open laptop. The mug of coffee alongside her had long since been emptied. Every so often she wrote something in a notebook. Was she a university student taking notes? He was intrigued to know. How long could he resist his desire to speak with her? He returned for a third day. She was nowhere to be seen.

A heartfelt, lost opportunity like so many others.

Mussels

Suzanne sat on a large log looking out to sea. The tide had fully retreated. It was one of the lowest spring tides of the year. Large patches of pungent sandy mud filled the spaces between the exposed rocks, acres of seafloor normally covered with plenty of water. She could see him in the distance, collecting the large blue-black mussels and depositing them into a pail. She had met him once before and he had invited her to accompany him once again, with the promise of a home-cooked meal afterward. Suzanne agreed with pleasure.

She was attracted to his well-developed muscles.

I Do

He’s a DJ, she's a music store clerk. Their increasingly intimate flirtation involved only music titles via WhatsApp. *Da Ya Think I’m Sexy* elicited a *Sexy Eyes* response. *I Can’t Get No Satisfaction* provided a *Relax* reply.

They eventually married with vows *I Do, I Do, I Do, I Do.*

A Legend

Oh, he was handsome alright - Hollywood handsome - with thick black hair, chiselled jaw, and a smile to melt hearts, which of course he frequently did. On each mission, he carried a lady’s heart and desire with him in the cockpit. Its owner changed from mission to mission. On his final sortie, her name was Diane.

How he piloted the damaged plane home remains a legend within the squadron. They extricated him from his seat unconscious. Surgery removed the irreparably damaged leg.

He counted his blessings; two crutches and her heart were all that he needed. He married Diane two months later.

Love's Name

I like it so very much
that you know my name
not just the name
the world calls me
or the one my mother used
when I transgressed
but a name that is in a language
from no known place
yet is in every place that we inhabit
the name that sums up
who I am in this world?
the name that only you and I speak
the name that only
intimacy can give
saying so much about
our journey, our joy, our pain

Early Autumn

Early autumn. The mid-morning sun streaks through the oaks, leaves partially dressed for fall, some green but many golden yellow, burnt orange, bright red. As the gentle breeze moves them the sunlight flutters on its path through the blinds onto the closed eyes of the resting figure on the couch. Behind those closed eyes fluttering light gives sparkle to the azure blue water. A woman is running barefoot on the sand to greet him.

Here's your tea Grandpa

He opens his eyes, reaches for his tea and wonders if, like her Grandma, she too will run to her soul mate.

Stone Skipping

It is a warm, windless, summer evening. It's high tide. The water's surface is calm, waveless, reflective, making a gentle wish, wash at the shoreline. John is at the water's edge picking up skipping stones.

For his first throw he says, *This is for you, Mum*. The stone skips five times.

This is for you, sweetheart (his wife). Skips four times.

This is for you, Dad. Skips twice.

This is for you, Mellissa (his first love). Skips seven times.

For his final stone he says, *And this is for me.* Skips once.

Is stone skipping a new means to measure love?

Cold Clay

Simone was motionless for thirty minutes at a stretch. She disclosed at the end of the session that she went into a meditative state. While she meditated, Bill moved clay to try and resemble her figure. In his mind, his hands massaged her soft, warm skin and not cold clay.

Contours

Philippe's day job was as a highly regarded photographer. He specialised in high-resolution drone images of the earth and nature's beauty, its landscapes, mountains, valleys, rolling hillsides.

In his free time, Philippe continued his passion for nature's beauty but as a geographer exploring the contours of the female form.

Lay Lady Lay

She lay beside him like so many times before, her life story written in the lines and creases on her face and stomach. He felt honoured to be part of that story. But he could no longer put off the inevitable. No more secrets. The front desk would call 911.

Masseuse

His visual world is reduced to a small circle of floor and portions of feet shoed in bright red canvas. It's a visual porthole made smaller when his head is depressed into the donut as she puts pressure onto his shoulders. He's constrained to just feeling and to thinking. Thinking that no human has explored his nakedness so fully before, not even his most energetic of lovers.

While the unseen masseuse is kneading body parts never before touched, he's trying to resist fantasizing about the red-shoed woman, becoming anxious about the consequences of the stirrings in his groin.

"Please rollover!"

Curious

I'm curious
what's it like to stand for the first time
naked in front of a stranger
or perhaps a first-time lover
long after the blush of youthful
inquisitiveness has passed
long since the skin was tight and stomach
flat
now owning a body showing an erotic
history
in its folds and rolls

There's a love of cakes, over nourishment
here a sign of childbearing,
or a scar of medical intrusion
and weakened muscles
smelling of cologne rather than youth
such intimacy is surely rife for anxiety

And what of he, with belly distended
Adonis, he's not, abs now but a memory
will he still perform as he hopes?
will they achieve the joy they both seek?
so much anxiety to overcome

Waiting

Long ago they had been lovers but somehow drifted apart; each eventually marrying someone else. They both realised their mistake.

In the intervening years they remained friends, managing to meet for an illicit reunion once a year.

They agreed to wait until their respective offspring had reached adulthood before seeking divorce.

Stroke

It was a stroke of luck.

Stan bumped into his old flame at the grocery store.

His stroke of good fortune continued. She accepted his invitation to coffee.

He learned she too was unattached. They agreed to see each other again.

Both of their partners had succumbed to a stroke.

Love Feast

You offered up your love to me
That we could dine on
a three-course meal of affection

For starters
purely to arouse
you undress
the appetizer of naked skin
lightly tanned, sweetly fragrant
beneath a painted
ripe tomato red pout of desire

For dessert you reserved
your breasts
proud on their
soft, pale coloured platter
topped with pink, pert buds

You saved till last
your femininity

Nothing *inter*
about this
the *main* course
embellished
with three small
come hither tattoos

Three Michelin stars?

5 – State of Mind

Pills

Before bed, I swallow some new pills in order to bring me some sunshine. The old pills seem only to induce unpleasant, unwanted side effects, without blowing the clouds away. With high expectations, I'll wait until morning to see if these replacements are effective.

But for now, the sun sleeps.

Disappearing

Every time someone made a decision for him, without consultation, he disappeared. In the early years, disappearance manifested as a mental withdrawal. Later, a cabin in the woods became a place to retreat, one he controlled.

When he was made redundant his disappearance got serious.

The police never found him.

The Shadow

His former life had become a tethered shadow, pulling him back toward destructive and unhealthy outcomes. One dark winter's night he'd had enough. He took decisive action; spoke to it; firmly disowning it; setting himself free of his past. By summer's sunshine, the shadow obediently followed. They both left town.

Good Enough

His internal narrative said, "*You are not good enough.*" It was a remnant from his early life and flew in the face of feedback and accolades from family and friends as an adult.

Thankfully, on one occasion his narrative was true. He botched his suicide and got help he needed.

Adrift

Every weekend he escaped the considerable land-based stress he suffered and immersed himself in the concerns of the wind and tide. Sailing was a passion. Being surrounded by water was his joy. One Monday his boat was found adrift. The skipper was nowhere to be found.

He'd left a note.

Addiction

In the morning it's essential to have a strong coffee. In the evening it must be a glass or two of wine. In between its cigarettes; smartphone; Facebook; Fox News; more coffee; snacks; tea; biscuits; reefers; acetaminophen; anti-depressants.

Are we a species addicted to more than we care to admit?

Bill's Likes

It seemed Bill always had an obsession. If he liked something, he simply could not get enough.

As a boy, when the jar had cookies he liked, he binged until it was empty.

When adult, he favoured beer and women.

Inevitably, he had multiple marriages, infidelities and finally, liver disease.

Prognosis

He had an inkling it was going to be a long wait, so he brought along a book to read. Not that he could concentrate on reading. They'd been friends with since high school; lovers since university. Depending on today's prognosis he faced the daunting prospect of becoming her caregiver.

How Do You Do That

How did the most curious of questions "*How do you do that?*" become received as an implied instant criticism - "*You do it wrong?*" It's such an impediment to any relaxed conversation. An impediment with historic origin. The source probably a critical parent or schoolteacher, now hard-wired into the adult psyche.

Without Bars

Parents and society set the pattern. Up early to go to school, then to college and then to work. It was not until his fiftieth birthday that he realized no one had asked him what he wanted. He'd not even asked himself.

Now with responsibilities he felt imprisoned without bars.

First

First of the twins born, he endeavoured to be first thereafter. The first family member to graduate, first amongst his peers to get married, first to get divorced. At work he strived, becoming CEO.

Amongst his peers there was one thing he wanted to be last at - his demise.

Zero-Sum

Ultimately, it was a zero-sum game that he lost. Actually, he did not really lose; he just had no resolve to enter the contest. She got everything - as she put it - as "retribution for the years of support and sacrifice to you and the kids."

Now, he was living, or rather existing, with the indignities that came from no permanent address, no place to attend to personal hygiene. It was a hell of price to pay for his own sacrifice to a job that demanded so much but in return paid for food and mortgage.

The bottle deadened his anger.

Invisible Man

He's always there
tethered to me
I look around
cannot see
the scope of him

He hides always
this invisible man
but his presence
enduring, omnipotent

I do something
he chides
don't this, do that
it's not good enough

Or me

The Shoulds

A wall free, barless
stockade called the ISD[17]
enclosed with
rhetorical razor wire
constructed of rules
expectations

Its warden
sits on the shoulder
to keep the unruly in check
the animal tamed
incarcerating the me from me
so the me I might be
accords with social mores

I should be
more fit, less fat
more polite, less stressed,
more wealthy, less serious
more empathetic
more, less whatever….??

Does the list ever end?
if and when it does
the ad man comes along
decides some new shoulds
brighter teeth, sweeter breath
more mojo, newer car

Seeds for anxiety

---

17 *"I Should Do"*

prospective ground for
the medical industry
plus, their friends in big pharma
or the psychological
self-help industry

Each offering their own shoulds
antidotes to resolve my shoulds
should exercise
should meditate
should do yoga
should take Wellbutrin

But why should I give a damn?
should I not by now
have earned the right to
give the finger
to the warden
and all his dictates?

Should I find the courage
I should be uncaged

Tomorrow's Resolutions

Each night he was an insomniac; laying there, waiting for sleep; sleep that was just one more thought away, then another, and another. Yet, in the daylight, he sleepwalked through his days, his weeks, his years. Robotically he lived his life. Robotically he avoided being consciously present in his life. In the morning he resolved he would do something, just as he had resolved yesterday and the day before and the day before that. Then his bedside phone rang. The caller said his father had suddenly died. It took but a simple phone call to give tomorrow's resolutions a new urgency.

Scream

Munch surely knew it
a scream is a powerful thing
like a left hook onto a boxer's bag

The vocal exhalation
or the punch
give momentary escape
to the demons within

Have you ever wanted to scream?
scream so loud, so out of control
scream because
no carefully considered speech
does justice to the pain
you feel better afterward don't you?
I declare if there is not *Scream Therapy*
there should be
talk therapy, writ large!

6 – Nature's Pleasures

Water to a Whale

The environment. Everything around us, within us. Water to a whale. Air to an albatross. Earth to an earwig. So essential yet so unseen. Like dripping water torture, we alter it; slowly consume it. It has no voice. Its only response is to deprive us of life as we sleepwalk.

Starstruck

A warm August night drew out the crowds to see the show. Just as on the nights before, the audience was enthralled. The performance was flawless, standing out from the other named stars. Some used opera glasses for a closer view.

Technically, it was not a star but a comet.

Pink

Brightly coloured Riviera buildings reach skyward, pink, orange, and red walls with terracotta roofs. Pale, scantily clad bodies lay on the sand, turning pink and red in the bright Mediterranean sun. Perhaps the buildings were originally pale, but now are coloured from standing, without sunscreen, for years in the sun?

Fire

In the cold winter's air chimneys puff aromatic clouds. The wood smoke and their summertime cousin – bonfires – with smouldering leaves and yard clippings, elicit comforting aromas.

Likewise, fire-cooked food is entwined with man's existence. Ask campers around an open fire or a man flipping BBQ burgers. Banning flame diminishes life.

Winter

Sitting on the porch listening, the warm evening breeze envelops me, nurtures me, speaks to me, calms me.

Be warned, breeze says, *soon my cousin from the north will come and bite you. Prepare yourself, your home, chop more wood, can more food. It will be a long, white winter.*

Moonlight

The forest creaks: speaks to itself until the snow gently falls. Then, a bright white silence envelops everything. It's a time not to speak, but to look, to reflect, to feel. Winter brings a cold, peaceful magic to the soul if only we care to listen. Our missteps leave tracks.

Sounds Afloat

A plop, plop comes from the tethered dinghy, indicating the slightest of swells, while a wish, wash comes from wavelets arriving on the nearby pebbly beach. A pita, pita, pita of the gentle rain on the cabin roof keeps me inside.

All are comforting sounds, anchored in a safe bay.

Rain

Rain. A distant memory. Sixty days dry. Lawns - yellowed straw. Car washes, sprinklers banned. Two months since the sweet fragrance of fresh, light rainfall suffused nostrils. More since the drumming of droplets was heard on windowpanes, tin roofs. Thunder - so long ago its memory almost lost.

The new sound of the natural world is the incessant clicking of cicadas.

That naked dance enjoyed in the warm summer rain. When will we have that pleasure again?

Temperate cultures slowly learn to become desert peoples. For air-con manufacturers and carrion a god-sent opportunity.

For everyone else, a lethargy-inducing furnace.

El Nino

The air continued to hang heavy, sticky, damp, oven hot. It had been like this for months. The Humidex was off the scale. The Governor ordered all work, public activity cancelled. Air conditioners were allowed for only two hours per day. The grid was overloaded. Electrical usage was enforced - smart meters caught those who deviated.

At home, ceiling fans and nakedness were the closest thing to comfort. Even scrotums could no longer keep cool. Male fertility plummeted - not that many couples had the desire to copulate in such heat. El Nino made otherwise illegal immigration welcome. IVF clinics prospered.

Morning Ritual

The household chimneys puff their smoke. So too does the snowy mountaintop, puffing its dirty white cloud downwind until the rising sun washes away the grey, whitens the clouds, momentarily lighting up the mountain with a luminous yellow glow.

It’s a winter’s morning ritual that raises the human spirit.

Leaves to Remember

It is not the orange
nor the backlit yellows
offset by pines of green

Nor is it the blood-red maple
that catches the eye and
make us gasp

It is not the backdrop
blue and flawless

Nor the virginal houses
with imagined romances
set under cool porches

It is not the Fall
but the volume

The extent of Autumn
of all this colour

These hues forced upon us
by nature's palette

On tilted hills and at every turn
that is so unavoidably inspiring

Bull Frog 2 AM Insomnia

Those bloody fellows bleat
carefully timed
to match
my own heartbeat

Incessant is their throating,
rasping, gasping
all through the night
until the early morn

No more, no more
I implore

No more mating
no more mooing
it's going to be
your undoing

Enough, be done
you buggers
I'm in need of sleep

Silence or else
it's going to be
a twenty-two
with night scope
for you

Wiltshire

The landscape gently rises up towards the hill. An ancient dry-stone wall separates a field of yellow rape to one side from a field of green pasture on the other. Near the stone wall stands a solitary, ancient oak tree, not yet in full leaf; its branches reaching skyward, fingers open to catch the sun to feed its burgeoning shoots. On the green pastured hillside is a large white horse; topsoil artistically removed to expose white chalk, creating an equine image viewable for miles. A majestic red-tailed kite swoops low, hunting for small creatures unwisely exposed.

Beautiful Wiltshire countryside in April.

Stones

She walks slowly barefoot
eyes down
every so often stooping
to pick up a pebble
with colour or shape meaning something
adding to her collection
while the gentle swells
swish back and forth
back and forth
smoothing edges of angular stones
one against the other
with a noise of a muted rattle

What do these water-honed stones
hold for her?

Slack Tide

The surface
oily and silent
languidly creeps forward
is it water or sky?
the dripping greyness
has made each
imperceptible
from the other

Drip by drip
this moisture reaches into
my being
calmness, quietness
overwhelms me.

The peacefulness soothes
while somewhere near
a loon breaks the silence
with a haunting,
strangely comforting
sound

Seaweed
other flotsam
slowly float landward
pebbles disappear
a moment when
all is still
the tide is slack

West Coast Mornings - The View

All colour has been
sucked by the overcast grey
leaving
the water
barely perceptible
from the statuesque heron
on steely guard
for his next meal

In the far distance
shadowy mountains
wear an unruly, dirty white cloud
as scarfs and turbans
while booms of lumber
await in the foreground
their fate to become the paper
upon which to record the scene

Just then, to my right
a tear opens
a torchlight of sun appears
turning melancholy to hope
while to the north the cloud
has now absorbed the sea
its existence only confirmed by
a faintly visible vessel
moving from left to right
silently traversing between
hidden parcels of land

Seaside Medicine

Cool breath from the water
chills the overstressed fever
of workaday life

The Wish-wash sounds
on the pebbled shoreline
soothe the noisy mind

Pungent, pickled seaweed
baking in the sun
produces its unique
aroma therapy

All heal without prescription
or pharma logical intervention

X7

X7 sang out to his group. He'd seen and suffered enough. It was time to act. "We will retaliate, target small craft, do everything to prevent loss of life but collateral damage may be unavoidable," he sang. "Nature's passivity will not be taken for granted."

In packs they sought out their prey, moving speedily in unison, creating a wake that overturned small boats. Unfortunately, those aboard without PFD's paid heavily for their foolishness.

Scientists scratched their heads at this new behaviour. Orcas were known aggressors of seals. Now the same hunting skills were being directed towards man, disruptors of their environment.

Choo

Choo, choo, choo
Piercing call

Caw, caw, caw
Answers

White gull to blackbird

Each with its own language

Maw, maw, maw
says another unseen

It's a peaceful, noisy,
multi-ethnic bird world

Are birds multi-lingual?
Is there need to understand the call of
others?

Perhaps not
until the eagle appears

7 – Ageing

Public House

One of two magnets for the small village community, welcoming places where viewpoints, grumbles, solutions to world problems are aired; where local gossip is exchanged, all lubricated with a pint of ale or perhaps a gin and tonic.

Locals, characters, bon vivants meet each week at The Crown, Public House.

Plein Aire[18]

She stands in the southern heat

forcing pigment into pigment
before it dries so swiftly in the breeze
trees emerge, shadows, a lake perhaps
still to be revealed before dinner calls
or the arthritic knees cry foul
and demand reprieve.

[18] In Huatulco, Mexico, 2018

Pursuit

On her front porch swing, Marie sat accompanied by only her memories. Memories of her youth in Andalusia, the dancing, the music, all the handsome young men that pursued her.

Marie's only pursuer now was her dog and that nuisance estate agent wanting her to sell her property for development.

The Boundary

The boundary had been a long-standing bone of contention between them.

Beautiful, manicured lawn and flower beds existed on one side of the fence.

Unruly vegetables and weeds on the other.

Their dispute had been both rancorous and vocal.

When eventually he passed away, she and the fence were unmoved.

The Care Home

Had it been twelve hours? Time marked by the taking of medications.

No job to clock in; clock out.
No train to rush and catch.
No Fridays to crave.
No vacations to yearn or plan.

Each day like all the others.

Life now languished between his meals and his pills.

Tinnitus

Sitting in his window seat, eyes closed, he's warmed by the early morning sun recalling being warmed on pristine beaches. His coffee gets colder. Back then he heard a soothing lapping of waves.

Now, he hears an electrical transformer humming in his ears, a constant background to his current life.

Mustang

Jim's now proud owner of a beautiful, fully restored, lipstick-red, Mustang convertible with cream leather seats. It's a car he's desired ever since life seemed to end, when, long ago, the attractive blonde he tried to date became girlfriend of a Brylcreemed, dark-haired rival, owner of a similar car.

Unfortunately, that outcome predicted his ongoing lack of success with women.

Now, his luck was going to change!

To his surprise, the attention he received with his new wheels came mostly from other men.

Were they reminiscing about pretty girls from the past who wanted rides in a red convertible?

Steed

Long ago he sat
astride his steed
a shiny, black,
hot-blooded, Arabian.

The only mane
one can see now
is his ponytail,
as if to recall
past hippie days
and some semblance of
retained virility.

Later on
his charger was
a red rag-top
an equine-badged
chick magnet.
302 cubic inches of
pulsating
testosterone.

Now, in life's final insult
to all his masculinity,
he rides a puny,
three-wheeled scooter.

On Being Seventy

Really!

what's there to celebrate?
seven decades
twenty-five thousand days
I can't comprehend
I've been here this long.

Like a Dali watch
this age feels, well,
flexible.
perhaps only noon
… in the worst case.

After all
it does not seem so long ago
when the age I am now
when seen back then
would appear
so bloody old!

It's true that,
like Cohen,
there are now aches in places I used to play
complaints frequently arise to my brain
from these places
a brain that refuses to acknowledge
the decades of its occupancy.

But entropy always happens
it's had

six hundred thousand hours
to make apparent those
disorders at the joints
and who knows where or what else
internally.

Shavings

Octogenarian Stan sat on his sunny porch, rugged up against possible chill. He had his favourite pocketknife in one hand, a yellow cedar whittling stick in the other. As he mused about his long life, he shaved away at the stick. Each shaving elicited a particular memory; his playful youth; army combat; the marriage to his high school sweetheart; their two children and grandchildren.

When his daughter dropped by later that afternoon, she found him slumped over, with a pile of wood shavings at his feet. She collected the shavings, later placing the memories alongside him in his casket.

Lost

It has to be here somewhere!

Rod's lost his watch. He's now wasting time searching.

Losing things is a recent habit – so is losing time looking for the lost object.

An invisible vortex is slowly devouring his possessions, his memory, his time – which at ninety-six is in very short supply.

This Body

This body
that sees
that grieves
that breathes

this body
that walks
that eats
that talks

this body
that bawls
that writes
that falls

this body
that sleeps
that dreams
that weeps

this body
that hugs
that loves
that shrugs

this body
that's old
that's tired
that's cold

this body
that's done
that's almost gone

Uncertainties

I now live with uncertainties
each wave of unease
crashes noisily onto my shore.

There is no holding them off
and I've yet to learn to surf.

So, I fall frequently
into a washing machine
of wet turmoil.

Crashing, foaming emotion
until
the storm passes
into warmth and calm.

It was not always thus.

For so long I held a youthful
assurance that
I only had to
think hard enough
analyse well enough
to tease
a solution to the problem.

Now the waves
reign supreme.

8 – Death & Disease

Kick Out of Life

In the fall, the boy kicked piles of oak leaves. In youth, he kicked a football on the local team.

In his teens, he was kicked out of school. In his twenties, he kicked a cigarette habit.

In his work, he kicked ass.

In his seventies, he kicked the bucket.

Angels

There was no diminishing her playfulness. Her smile and laughter were infectious. That winter, in the fresh snow, she made snow angels.

Presciently, it was her last time before she finally succumbed to the enormity of her illness.

She joined the angels… Angela RIP 1981-1993

Parkinson's

Before, a life well ordered, of leadership, control, and absence of surprises. When the unexpected occurred, mental acuity existed to resolve and recover. Such was the life before Parkinson's, before memory loss, before mobility challenges, before fatiguing drugs. Now, each week brings undeniable loss; grieving follows grieving as capability dies.

Cancer

Today, another friend has been diagnosed with cancer.

Soon, I won't know anyone without this modern malady. It's become the demise of so many of the health-conscious, post-war boomers.

Now, we're all living long enough for the reckless proliferation of rogue cells to have time to inflict their fatal destiny.

No Lyrics

There were no lyrics, only the strings of a classical guitar moved by the musician's fingers.

And yet; and yet the instrument clearly spoke a refrain, "*Go to him; Go to him.*"

She left the concert early, finding him on the floor.

Music and a first responder saved his life.

Demons

He wept alone with his demons, listening constantly to soothing, soft jazz.

One day demons got the upper hand. He pitched a can of baked beans at the window with the fury of a baseball. Glass and can landed on the street below.

It got attention. They changed his meds.

Coffee

They met Fridays for coffee. Six men. Retired. Sharing their afflictions. Seeking confirmation of views on the politics of the day, of the tattooed younger generation, of their troublesome offspring. Recording the passing of acquaintances.

Above all, hoping that there would still be six of them to meet next week.

Waiting for Her Husband

She had been waiting patiently for nearly eighteen months. Not that she wished for a short wait. He had every reason to enjoy his time without her, having put his life on hold to be her full-time caregiver.

The plot next to hers was reserved for when he was ready.

On Being Late

Being on time had been a perennial challenge for him. Family, friends knew to expect his late arrival. It was a stressful element when the family travelled together. On his last journey, road works, and traffic added delay.

The mourners were not surprised when the hearse arrived fifteen minutes late.

Diagnosis

The poet hears
looks to write something
of nature's circle of life.

The engineer hears
goes to calculate
what are the odds
what is the likelihood
of false negatives
of false positives.

A lover hears
weeps and wails
knowing, sensing
what will be lost.

A scientist hears
is assured
all is well,
confirming the cellular descent into chaos
the second law of thermodynamics.

For everyone
poet, engineer, lover
and scientist
there is this life
forever altered.

A Death Without Dying

He stood uneasy,
a shadow of his former self.

Not that there was any less to his bulk
nay…there was more of him than before
(an unpleasant side effect of the meds).

But he was nonetheless,
still ghostly and pale,
with sweat beaded on his brow
(another of those unpleasantries).

He watched intently
as parts of him
were lowered into the freshly dug hole.

First in went his Self
the Self as he knew it
the Self he'd constructed over seven
decades.

His wife, meanwhile
respectfully dressed in black
wailed, grieving uncontrollable sadness
as who he was
who they were
who they had been
was lowered into history.

His Libido followed his self
lowered beyond reach
and with it went all his dreams
of flesh upon flesh.

As tears flowed
on those ghostly cheeks
an even greater wail
escaped his lips.

His Control
despite its vocal resistance
was corralled
then lowered
and covered with soil.

All he was
was now gone.

All he knew of himself
was now history.

All he now presented
was a body.
An assemblage of organs
one of which
was soon to be shot
by a technician
with a beam of radiation
Its capital punishment
for a life of
reckless growth.

He was effectively dead
but was not dead.

Alive
but not alive.

Man
but not man.

Existing now it seems
as merely a target
for a medical sharpshooter.

The Power of Sickness

Alan found there was positivity to his recent bedridden illness. He discovered he had gained a certain power over his loved ones and his caregivers who responded favourably to his many requests in order to make him more comfortable in his discomfort. Alan no longer had to actively do anything. He only had to ask. It gave him time to think, to reflect, to sleep, and to bask in the filtered sunshine streaming through the window sheers. It all seemed a decadent luxury that Alan had not afforded himself during his adult life.

Unfortunately, it and his life would soon end.

The Gift

The date was neither Christmas, birthday nor anniversary. There was no box wrapped in red ribbon nor a card espousing good wishes. It was simply a piece of paper. Typed thereon was stated,

Normal. No abnormal or cancer cells present.

A huge gift despite the absence of wrapping and bows.

9 – Just for Fun

Aromatic Wood

The project did not matter. It was all about the aroma. The more sawdust produced; the more shavings he curled off the wood; the more his nostrils were filled with a smell that transfixed him into a Zen-like state.

On some days he was even known to make something useful.

White World

There's no need to pull back the drapes. The peaceful silence says it all. Plus being December. My immediate world has been blanketed overnight with sound-deadening insulation. Either white, winter's playground or treacherous territory, depending on your age. A noisy snowplough passes.

Oh! Where did I put the snow shovel?

Three of Them

After the pick-up and on the way home he wondered if there was going to be room for the three of them. But he was besotted. A ménage à trois it had to be. He opened the door. It was clearly love at first sight.

His wife adored the puppy.

Killing Me Softly[19]

The song still evoked such meaning. Smells and feelings arose immediately on hearing it. Where was he now, that young enigmatic lover who played her heart as romantically as his guitar?

He grew up, got a real job, losing something along the way.

He was presently making her breakfast.

Her Dad

A deceased life is in part defined by personal items left behind - books, art, pictures, photographs, writings. She was clearing out his house, opening her deceased father's laptop, reading his writings, emptying his night table.

OMG. Shock, horror!

It seems he was a sexual being … not just Dad.

Globes

Youthful Sam had a treasured bag full of the colourful tactile globes. They provided endless hours of competitive play with other boys. Years later, Sam pursued games with more serious outcomes at the casino.

When his daughter helped him move at age seventy, she became aware he'd lost his marbles.

---

[19] Killing Me Softly with His Song by Roberta Flack

Alexa

The voice-activated speakers were broadcasting meditation music. The vaporizer was puffing its fragrant mist of sandalwood. A steaming mug of lemon zinger sat on the counter. The bath was ready, the Epsom salts were dissolved. All set!

Except the emotions were not right!

Fuck: "*Alexa, play Bitch by Meredith Brooks.*"

Second Hand

It was her favourite pastime, cruising the second-hand markets looking for bargains. Her home was adorned with successful finds, some of which she had to refinish before they were displayed. It was no different for him.

Married twice before, he had to change his habits before he was presentable.

Landfill

Wednesday is bin day - the day that a specially designed vehicle collects detritus from a week's living for its journey to the landfill site.

Sunday, a specially designed vehicle collects cargo for its journey. Friends, relatives watch as a life's living is lowered into the earth at another site.

Under Control

Living alone. Intrusions only reflections in the windows; in the mirrors. An encapsulated world save for the ones imagined in the many books lining the library walls. Dining in silence except for the purring of Ginger the cat.

Everything in life neatly under control except … doorbell chimes. Her lover?

Windsor Frames

As librarian, Sam looked the part with Windsor framed spectacles. He spent his working hours surrounded by only whispered, hushed tones.

On weekends, he immersed himself with intense sound as the lead rock guitarist of Sammy G. and The Fender Benders. He still looked the part, with his Windsor frames[20].

[20] As worn by John Lennon

Sam's Wheels

Sam's life was curiously defined by wheels. His very first were on a push toy to help him walk; then it was a foot-propelled tricycle, then a three-wheeled pedal bike followed by a two-wheeler with training wheels. Eventually, he progressed to a normal bicycle, then a motorcycle. Ultimately, he acquired a car; one of many.

His love of wheels took him into driving professionally - an eighteen-wheeler and a forty-foot fifth wheel on vacation.

Years later, he loved to speed his electric scooter around the care home until he was wheeled out on a gurney.

Sam Wheeler RIP 11.09.2022

Girls[21]

I'm not interested in girls
he said, as he
strapped his fishing rod
to the crossbar
of his bike
and rode off to the beach.

The next time
before leaving
he was seen brushing his hair.

What was he fishing for?

[21] This is autobiographical, ca. 1963

Are You?

Are you in love?
and write of bliss
or not in love
so, write of search.

Are you platonically attached?
and write of friendship
or have lost love
so, write of grief.

Are you happily single?
and write of oneness
or unhappily alone
so, write of loneliness.

Are you devoid of ideas?
and write of emptiness
or emotionally flat-lined
so, write of stillness.

Are you reading poetry?
and write fresh rhymes
or listening to songs
so, write new lines.

Are you reading a book?
and write new prose
or observing nature
so, write of wonder.

Are you....??

But that's enough about you

because
YOU are but a proxy for ME

Today, I must write something
anything, without censure
just for my soul
for no one to see.

Forecast

Sipping morning coffee Jan heard the long-range forecast – above seasonal temperatures and rainfall. *That's about right, more heated arguments and tears*, she thought. Jan's current relationship had entered its final phase.

Oh, for a change in weather, a new lover, frequent sunny smiles with a chance of joyful tears.

Hurkle-Durkle[22]

Weekends were hectic. So many tasks needed to be squeezed into the two days to ensure that the subsequent work week went smoothly for the two of them. Both days were fully filled with grocery shopping, house cleaning and finding time to socialise with friends or family.

Perhaps John and Yoko set the example in Amsterdam[23]. Every month Sam and Joy booked a local hotel room for Saturday night. Sundays were spent in the room, in bed, with food delivered via room service.

As a widower, Sam revived this practice, but with room service covering more than his gastronomic needs.

---

[22] To Hurkle-Durkle = (Scots) to lie in bed or lounge about when one should be up and about.

[23] Bed-ins for Peace, Room 702, Amsterdam Hilton Hotel, March 25-31, 1969

Fast Food

Developed in partnership with multi-national take-out food chains, the newest, must have technology gadget is a plug-in device for smartphones. While watching TV the phone app simultaneously activates the device. Fragrant molecules are thus released inviting hunger in the user. The device is available for free. Fragrance refills come at a very nominal cost.

Production of the device can barely keep up with consumer demand. Smell-of-Vision has increased take-out profits. Food delivery services are prospering.

In contrast, revenue from fast-food advertising is plummeting now that there is a direct link to customer's olfactory senses rather than simply using visual cues.

Illustrations

Publishing History

Vines Leaves Press.com (50 Give or Take)

A Modern Life
Dog Walk
Water to a Whale
Mirror be Damned
Slumber
Coffee
Wedding Gift
Human being
Globes
Relationship Breakdown
Twenty-Six
Play
Silhouette

Wordstorm's Counterflow Magazine

Stones
Slack Tide

Sage-ing: The Journal of Creative Ageing

On Being Seventy
Steed
Diagnosis
The Gift
A Death without Dying
Writing
What is Poetry?

Fiftywordstories.com

Aromatic Wood
Times Change

101Words.org

Mussels
The Drink

Vancouver Island Regional Library's Sea and Cedar Magazine

West Coast Mornings – The View

About the Author

Before qualifying to be an engineer there were hints of my interest in creative writing. A poem here, a short creative piece there, usually written to meet some course requirements.

For the following thirty-six years my working life required me to write proposals seeking higher level, technical and financial approval. Those documents were always structured in a consistent format so as to suit corporate processes. Along with the proposals were detailed, line by line, instructions for the execution of what was proposed. Occasionally, there was a need to write longer reports, outlining the analysis and the technical and financial rationale for a particular course of action – so called "Technical Writing".

Once retired, and in stark contrast to my working life, I sought out creative art forms, pottery, sculpture and free verse poetry. I found the freedom to write without strict rules compelling.

In 2022, I discovered Flash Fiction[24]. Specifically, the genre of very short stories – micro-fiction – written to an exact limit of, for example, 50 or 101 words. I became attracted

---

[24] From Wikipedia: Flash fiction, also called minimalist fiction, is a fictional work of extreme brevity that still offers character and plot development. Identified varieties, many of them defined by word count, include the six-word story; the 280-character story (also known as "twitterature"); the "dribble" (also known as the "minisaga," 50 words); the "drabble" (also known as "microfiction," 100 words); "sudden fiction" (750 words); "flash fiction" (1,000 words); and "microstory".

Some commentators have suggested that flash fiction possesses a unique literary quality in its ability to hint at or imply a larger story.

to the genre. It was (is) fun to write a very short story and then move on to write another one.

At about the same time, I started *The Posse* writing group which provided support and encouragement for the writing efforts of its members. A number of my written pieces, both fifty-word stories and poetry, were accepted for online publication, providing me with even further encouragement to keep writing.

This book reflects my writing passion. Within these pages are predominantly adult-themed short stories of more or less 50 words. Many of the pieces came from a personal challenge I set for myself in 2023 – fifty pieces of fifty words in fifty days.

The stories reflect my wry observations, sense of humour, and curiosity about the world around me.

It is an evocative, playful and at times dark compendium of stories and poetry that speaks to the nature of our lives, its high and lows, our pain and joy, our desires and losses, life's quirks and realities and even a bit of its silliness.

Manufactured by Amazon.ca
Bolton, ON

38262097R00076